Edna Hibel

Stories that Warm the Heart

D0104713

Edna Hibel

Stories that Warm the Heart

STARGROUP

Art by: Edna Hibel
Cover Art: Detail of *Mother and Child in Bliss,* oil and gold leaf on silk.
by Edna Hibel

Designed and produced by Star Group International, Inc.,
West Palm Beach, FL 33401
www.stargroupinternational.com

Library of Congress Catalog Card Number: 98-89214.

Edna Hibel: Stories That Warm The Heart
ISBN 1-884886-05-1

☆
STARGROUP

Printed in the United States of America

Table of Contents

Table of Contents

Preface

People often think of artists as leading solitary lives, working alone in their studios for weeks on end, emerging only for an occasional appearance at an exhibition. But internationally renowned artist Edna Hibel is nothing like the stereotype. Although it is not unusual for Edna to put in fourteen hours a day on her artwork, she has learned how to stay in touch with her friends and family while she works. Years ago, she trained herself to be able to talk while she is painting. She talks to friends and family on the phone, she talks to visitors to her studio, and she talks while giving painting demonstrations for her admiring fans. She simply loves interacting with people whenever possible.

During her demonstrations, patrons not only love for the artist to explain the techniques she uses to produce her works, they always ask her to tell her stories, for Edna has had some incredible adventures. Patrons who long to believe in the goodness of mankind and to revel in the beauty of the world around them find inspiration as Edna informally chats about her life. Her humanitarian philosophy always shines through in her unique and uplifting recollections.

This book is a long-overdue tribute to the artist as a story-teller, for it is the first time many of Edna Hibel's stories have been preserved in written form. It is also only the beginning—for this vibrant, down-to-earth artist will be honoring us with even more of her extraordinary tales in volumes yet to come.

X

The Early Years

Chapter 1

Early Creativity

Are creative people born or made? The nature/nurture debate will probably never be settled, but one thing is for sure: Edna Hibel demonstrated a creative nature very early in her life, even when she was a child playing.

Edna loved playing on the beach when she was young. She especially enjoyed building elaborate sand castles and digging deep holes. Once she clearly remembers sitting at the bottom of a hole so deep that she could look up and watch other parents grab their own children to keep them from falling in. She was fascinated by the perspective afforded her from her vantage point, and loved observing the world differently.

When she wasn't looking up from her holes, she was engrossed on seeing how far down she could see. Edna explains that whenever she dug deep holes, she imagined that she was digging her way to China. She had listened carefully when her parents told her that China was on the other side of the world. "One time I almost made it!" she relates. "I had this really deep hole dug and actually thought I felt a little hand shaking mine coming up from the bottom. It was really exciting!"

Little did Edna know that in later life she really would get all the way to China—but by plane, not by shovel.

Standing Out in a Crowd

Edna never appears to be nervous or bothered when people surround her to watch the painting demonstrations her fans love so well. In fact, she can't remember a time when she was nervous in front of a crowd. Perhaps her childhood prepared her for the adoring fans.

When she was only three, Edna began dance classes, quickly and enthusiastically mastering a type of acrobatic dancing. Soon her mother began taking her all over Boston to Women's Club meetings as the entertainment. It was so much fun. Edna never remembers having stage fright, but she does remember loving the applause.

Later, as a teenager, she would invariably attract crowds when she did her watercolors outdoors. People staring at her as she painted never bothered her, but animals sometimes did. Once a cow grazing nearby started lapping up her water before he could be shooed away, and another time a chicken managed to stick his beak into her paint. "That poor bird," Edna recalled, "He darted all over the yard trying to get the paint off him! I felt terrible, but he was too fast for me."

Another time, as she was painting, she felt eyes upon her. She turned around and there was a duck, sitting on her eggs. "I think she would have killed me if I had touched her or the egg," she recalls. "She looked furious!" Edna had been warned never to go near swans, geese, or ducks when she was out painting because they bite. The artist quietly left the protective mother and continued her painting elsewhere— without her overly critical audience of one.

The most difficult painting situation Edna can remember is when she wanted to paint a Russian dancer who was not allowed to leave the theater in her costume. Always determined, Edna set up her canvas to paint back stage. Whenever the dancer came off the stage, she would pose for Edna. Meanwhile, all the other dancers dashed back and forth as they were called on stage for their parts.

Deep in concentration, none of the confusion around her bothered Edna. That is, until one of the dancers ran right into her canvas, smashing it into her face! But even gooey paint on her face and smock was not enough to discourage the artist, who wiped off the paint and started reworking her ruined strokes. Despite the chaos, the painting turned out fine. Today, the dancer's portrait radiates the same serenity that has become Hibel's trademark.

People admiring the painting would never guess how the artist put herself into that work.

No Creativity Here

After graduating from high school, Edna Hibel's talent led to her enrolling in the School of the Boston Museum of Fine Arts. As a budding artist, she was creative and enthusiastic, always wanting to try new artistic techniques and media. Unfortunately, some teachers she encountered did not share Edna's enthusiasm.

When Edna first began art school at the School of the Boston Museum of Fine Arts, she was disappointed to find that she could not work a ceramics class into her very full schedule. Anxious to try this medium, she was thrilled to find that a class was being offered by the local YWCA. She signed up immediately.

The first day in the class she immersed herself in the joy of creating a figure in clay, but she was suddenly roused from her concentration when she felt someone staring at her. "What do you think you're doing?" the teacher bellowed sternly.

"Making a figure," was Edna's puzzled answer.

"But you are only allowed to make ashtrays in this class!" the teacher replied. "You can finish that one and fire it, but then you must leave."

Luckily for art lovers, Edna left after the figurine was completed—and in all these years has never done an ashtray. The figurine, however, remains with her to this day, a reminder of her rebellious days of youth.

Hibel Style

When strangers not familiar with Edna Hibel's work ask her to explain her style of art, she politely declines. Years ago, she learned that pictures say a thousand words, and that it's much better to let them do the talking.

When Edna married Tod Plotkin, she began to combine being a wife and homemaker with having a career. It was a struggle, especially after she gave birth to her first child. She really needed to establish herself as a professional, but it was slow going. Then, after a successful Boston exhibition, she was introduced to Mrs. McKinley Helm, the wife of a well respected art critic and writer. Mrs. Helm, very impressed with Edna's work, arranged for Edna to meet her husband.

Edna was thrilled. This was just the jump-start her career needed, but the meeting turned out to be a disaster. She had not thought to bring a single canvas. Helm therefore had to ask Edna to tell him about some of her paintings.

Edna gamely began describing a few of the paintings she had done in Mexico. Helm's reaction was not enthusiastic.

In fact, he condemned her work sight unseen, saying that he would probably hate it.

Edna left the meeting feeling crushed, but fate intervened in what might have been a setback for her budding career. A few weeks later, Mr. Helm happened to walk into a framing shop at the same time Edna's mother was there with two of her paintings. He had no idea who had done them, but Helm loved what he saw, and asked about the artist.

Before long Edna received a phone call from the apologetic Mr. Helm. He not only wrote a wonderful review of Edna's work, he also wanted to purchase both the paintings he had seen.

Although one of the two paintings Helm wanted was already sold, he did buy the other one. It is the only family portrait Edna has not kept for herself. A portrait of Jon, her firstborn son, now hangs in Helm's museum in Santa Barbara, California.

Edna learned a lot from the Helm experience. She vowed never again to try to explain her art style. The most she will say if she is pressed is that some have called her a "contemporary impressionist".

In the review of Edna's work, Helm himself stated that she had found "her signature"—her own style of art—at a very young age. "I guess I should say my style is Hibel," Edna laughs.

Is There an Artist in the House?

When Edna went into labor with her last son, Richard, little did she suspect that she would end up not only with a new baby, but also with a most unusual artistic experience—all because she trusted another professional's expertise. Her philosophy is, "If you're going to go to a doctor, trust him. I let people do their business."

It all began when Edna arrived in labor at a Boston hospital. Her doctor, who had been anxious to find a patient who would consent to letting him try out a new technique, asked Edna if she would be his guinea pig. He wanted to inject her with a pain killer to make childbirth less painful. Edna agreed, trusting that her doctor would certainly know more about medicine than she.

The procedure seemed to work well, and Richard came into the world hours later with no ill effects. Mother and baby were resting comfortably, but only until the next day, when

the doctor came rushing into her hospital room to ask a favor. It seemed that he had a second "guinea pig" ready to deliver in an adjoining room. The problem was, he needed someone to document the exact sites of the injections he would be giving. He knew Edna was an artist, and that she never went anywhere without her sketch pad and pencils.

Sure enough, new mother Edna had come prepared. Soon she was being whisked down the hall in a wheelchair to attend the delivery. She quickly sketched the woman's front and back sides as the doctor deftly administered the injections and then brought another beautiful new baby into the world.

Six months later, the doctor's article was published in the prestigious *New England Journal of Medicine*, illustrated by none other than Edna Hibel. You just never know when an artist will come in handy!

The Last Resort

Edna and Tod did not always live a charmed life. As with most young couples, there were times that they were quite worried about their finances. The lowest point in their financial history came when the Plotkin family business went bankrupt. It was before Edna had established herself as an artist, so she and Tod were desperate. She immediately started teaching art, charging two dollars a lesson, but that amount of money would hardly be enough to keep the family afloat.

There was a time, many years ago, when Tod and his brothers lost everything. The Plotkins used all their savings to try to save their women's specialty shops, but all efforts failed, and they had to close one retail outlet after another. Even Edna and Tod's house was in danger of being sold, since they had mortgaged it to try to keep the stores going.

It was during this financial crisis that Edna took comfort in knowing that if all else failed, she had five fur coats she could sell to bring in some money. Edna was hardly a clothes horse. In fact, she rarely wore any of them. They had been given to her years before by her father, who was a furrier. Now she realized that the coats might serve to put food on the table.

Before any sale was arranged, Edna got a call from her mother. Lena explained that her friend Frieda desperately needed a fur coat. Would Edna mind giving her one? Of course not. Edna happily gave away a Persian lamb coat to keep her mother's friend warm.

A few weeks went by and Edna received another call. Her cousin was about to go to school in Boston, and had no winter coat. Edna couldn't imagine going through a Boston winter without a heavy coat. Another fur coat to the rescue, and a happy cousin went to school warm.

Only a few days later a friend of Edna's asked to borrow her other Persian lamb coat. Edna thought she was lending it, but the lamb never found its way back to her door.

Soon another one of her mother's friends was declaring bankruptcy and was desperate for a warm coat. Edna came to the rescue, with a gorgeous mink coat for the distraught woman.

In two months time, Edna's stash of five coats had been reduced to one mink. At that point, she got a call from a friend who asked her out to a fancy restaurant. She wondered if she could borrow one of Edna's furs for the evening. Edna accompanied the woman that night wrapped in an old woolen coat with patches on the sleeves, while her friend luxuriated in the last of the furs.

"Edna," the friend later chided, "How can you wear that ratty old coat? Aren't you embarrassed to be seen in public?" Edna was speechless.

A Gallery for Mother – A Museum for Edna

Love has always played a major role in Edna Hibel's life —love of beauty, love of art, and love of family and friends. She cares a lot about those she loves, and in turn, a lot of people care about her. Sometimes, the love that radiates from her paintings and her personality inspires admirers in most unexpected ways.

When Edna's father passed away, her mother was devastated. Previously a very active person, Lena Hibel just gave up on living. Edna and Tod were quite concerned when they found they couldn't get her interested in anything.

Just as they were at their wit's end, someone offered Edna an old store in Rockport, Massachusetts for a gallery. Edna was skeptical, not having any idea how to run a gallery. Then, in the middle of the night, she woke up with a great idea. "Tod!" she exclaimed, "If Mama thought we needed her, we could get this gallery and have her run it. It will cost us $800, and I know we can't afford it, but it will be worth it!" A sleepy Tod agreed.

At six in the morning, Edna could wait no longer. She excit-edly dialed Lena's number and told her of the wonderful opportunity they had, if only Lena would agree to run the gallery. Her mother agreed, saying, "Well, if you need me..."

Never one to procrastinate once inspired, Edna signed the lease that day, and got her mother busy getting the gallery in shape. Lena plunged right in at a furious pace.

Although she had never run a business before, Lena had always been supportive and proud of her daughter's art. Her main concern, though, was what to charge for the paintings. They were already marked from $50 to $150, but Lena thought that was exorbitant. When she told Edna that she wouldn't have the nerve to ask that, Tod became quite adamant. He explained that when people questioned the prices, she absolutely could not go below what they were marked. "You can give them away, but don't ever sell them for less than they are marked," he directed.

But Lena was still not convinced. The first day the gallery opened, she called Tod to plead with him to let her sell a painting for less than it was marked to a nice couple who could not afford it. Tod did not budge, and the very next day an amazed Lena sold the painting at the full asking price. That encouraged her to stick with the prices on the tags.

Lena's education was just beginning. The second day on the job, Mr. and Mrs. Clayton Craig, who had come to Rockport to buy some oranges, wandered in to see the gallery. They immediately fell in love with the paintings, and chose five to purchase. Lena was ecstatic, but there was a problem. They said they had to go home to get some money. Always a trusting soul, Lena told the Craigs that they could go ahead and take the paintings, and bring the money to her later. They were flabbergasted. "How do you know you can trust us?" they asked. "With faces like yours," Lena explained, "I would trust you with anything." Edna's art had won their admiration, but Lena had won their hearts. They promptly returned with their checkbook.

For the rest of their stay, they came to the gallery almost every day, and with them came an amazing array of friends and colleagues, for Mr. Craig was the Chairman of the Board of the Christian Science Church. The Craigs felt that Edna Hibel's paintings expressed what they believed in, love and peace, and they continued to buy her works and promote her to their friends all that summer.

Three years went by with the Craigs' purchases continuing and their relationship with Lena better than ever, but something was very odd. As much as they adored Edna's paintings, the Craigs repeatedly refused to meet her. One day they explained to Lena why they did not want to meet her daughter. They had found that many of the other artists whose work they collected were disappointing in person,often being arrogant and snobby. They didn't want any personality faults they assumed Edna might have to take away from the beauty they saw in her paintings.

But despite the Craigs' reservations about Edna, the overdue meeting finally happened. Lena mentioned to the couple that Edna was getting an exhibit ready to send to Connecticut. Those were the magic words. Until then, the Craigs had seen everything that the artist had painted. Now they risked losing a chance to purchase some new works, and they couldn't stand missing out on such an opportunity. They meekly asked if they could visit Edna in her home to see the paintings, promising not to take too much of her time.

They arrived that day at about 2:00 p.m., chose a few pieces that they wanted, and then ended up staying for dinner at Edna's insistence. The "brief" visit lasted till 10:00 p.m. The next day, Mrs. Craig called Edna. She explained that she and Clayton had a wonderful home, full of beautiful furniture and art, but that she would give up everything they had for the feeling that was in Edna and Tod's house.

As a follow-up, one of Edna's young children asked his mother if the Craigs could come to dinner every night. Edna said, "I don't know. Why don't you write and ask them?" He did.

His letter was simple but heartfelt. "Dear Mr. And Mrs. Craig: Could you come to dinner every night? I love you." The friendship was cemented, with the Craigs coming to dinner often, and bringing many other art lovers, who ended up purchasing Hibels.

Soon after that initial visit, the Craigs traveled to the South of France and visited the Renoir Museum. They were shocked to find only one small original Renoir, and that one on loan, because all the other Renoirs were in private collections or in museums. They decided that they would never let that happen to Hibel's works, and pledged to continue to buy as much of her artwork as possible to eventually open a museum. When they returned and told Edna their idea, she was astounded, but the Craigs were determined. They even convinced Edna to start the Edna Hibel Art Foundation to assure that the paintings they had already acquired would go to a museum if they died before achieving their dream.

By 1976, the Craigs had amassed 180 original Hibels and 200 lithographs, but just when they were ready to build the museum, Mr. Craig had a change in fortune. No longer rich, the Craigs were not sure if they could even keep the collection.

Luckily, Edna had just begun making profitable collector plates. She told Mr. Craig that she was ready and willing to donate all the proceeds from her next plate to start the museum. Tod was incredulous, thinking they could not afford such a thing, and having no idea what the yet unplanned plate would even be. But Edna, with her typical optimism, created the *Flower Girl of Provence*, which sold out fast and made a tremendous amount of money.

Thus, in 1977, the dream became a reality, with the Craigs' donated paintings and the building financed with a single wildly successful plate. The Hibel Museum stands today in Palm Beach, Florida as the only privately owned public museum dedicated to a living artist.

And it all began because a couple went to town to buy some oranges one sunny day in Rockport.

When The Going Got Tough

Edna Hibel has a history of reaching out and helping people. As a high school senior she came up with the idea of starting a scholarship fund for subsequent students instead of donating a senior class gift. Her idea caught on, and the money her class raised was matched for years by contributions from other teachers and students, and ended up providing a continuous source of scholarships for worthy students.

During the past thirty years, Edna has helped innumerable charities, including the American Leukemia Society, the Muscular Dystrophy Association, the Arthritis Foundation, the Epilepsy Foundation, Catholic Charities, the Make A Wish Foundation, Special Olympics, the Jewish Arts Foundation, and many others. She says she is especially fond of organizations that help women and children, and has often donated original works to help them raise funds. With all her good works, some people may not realize that there was a time when Edna and Tod were on the receiving end of someone else's good deed.

In the late 1950s, before Edna became established as an artist, Tod and Edna went bankrupt. "Every specialty store in Boston failed within two years," she recalls, "including the Plotkin shops." The worst part was that Tod and Edna were going to lose their house. A number of friends heard of their situation and wanted to lend them money to save their home, but they adamantly refused. "We didn't know when, if ever, we could repay them," Edna explains.

Then a friend's father, who insisted on meeting with them, put everything into perspective. He wanted to pay off their mortgage and let them stay in the house until they could repay him, even if it took years. When they looked shocked, the man explained that when he was a young man, he was about to lose his flower shop because he could not raise $50. None of his family or friends was willing to help, but a stranger paid the bill and his business was saved. From that day on, he had vowed that someday he, too, would help a stranger. "So, we were it," says Edna.

When he was in his 90's, whenever their Good Samaritan would see Tod or Edna, he would start crying. "Just think," he would say, "I had such an important part in your career."

"The strange thing was that he had a reputation as quite a tough guy," says Edna, "but that was sure a wonderful thing he did for us."

Edna and Tod had discovered that when the going got tough, tough guys came in handy.

Family and Friends

Chapter 2

Childhood Classmates Fall in Love

For years, Tod Plotkin and Edna Hibel have been a compatible team. Early in their marriage, Tod decided to free Edna from housework and the care of the children so she could concentrate on her painting. Then he began framing her paintings and supervising the galleries. Later, as her fame grew, Tod arranged trips for exhibitions, collaborated on books, and took charge of almost all the marketing of Edna's works. Naturally, most people think that Tod and Edna's partnership began after they were married, but actually they had been together even as children.

Although they were only acquaintances in seventh grade, Edna and Tod ended up sharing an important office that year. Tod started the year as room president, but one day when he was absent, the teacher appointed Edna as president. Thus, Tod was president for half the year, and Edna president the last half. "We are still debating how that happened," quips Tod.

Later, in high school, Tod was president of his graduating class, but that time Edna did not share the office with him.

"I voted for him, though," she states. "Of course, all the girls did because he was very popular, since he was an excellent athlete."

Edna and Tod did not actually start dating until after they graduated from high school. "We were both 17 years old, and even though I had known him slightly for years, there was a certain moment when I felt it was love at first sight," states Edna. Their families had rented cottages on Nantasket Beach. One day Edna walked down the street, heard some music, turned, and saw her future husband. "It was Tod, sitting on a porch, playing his clarinet. At that minute, I knew I was in love," she relates.

The problem was that Edna had a summer romance going with a boy named Georgie. When Georgie's mother got wind of Edna's change of heart, she scolded Edna severely, saying, "This is only an infatuation that you have for this Plotkin boy. You are perfect for Georgie."

"She was right about the infatuation part," says Edna, "she was just wrong about the length of it."

Within a week of Edna's falling for Tod, he wrote a song dedicated to her. His inspiration was seeing Edna crying, right after Georgie's mother had spoken sternly to her about dropping Georgie.

Today Edna still has the handwritten song from almost 65 years ago, and they both can recite the sweet lyrics by heart:

You must smile
'cause when you do
all the while I see in you
all the beauty of the stars in the sky.

Don't you cry
'cause if you do
then the sky will darken too,
and the sun will stop
shining on high.

Stately trees and tiny flowers
of Mother Nature,
and the bees and every other kind of creature
can't compare their every grace
with the sweetness of your face
when you smile and capture my poor heart.

Georgie was furious when he heard about Tod's poem. He quickly tried to win her back by writing a violin concerto in her honor, but it was too late. Edna's heart had been won by Tod.

There was, however, an even bigger problem. Georgie's folks had a large room which they had allowed Edna to use as a studio. All her paints and other supplies were there when she fell for Tod. "That was ticklish," she says, with a twinkle in her eye.

Somehow, Edna managed to retrieve her paintings and brushes. Georgie may have been dispensable, but her art supplies? Never!

The Endless Courtship

Although Edna fell in love instantly with Tod that day she saw him in Nantasket, the courtship itself was rather prolonged. "In those days, we were too young to really date," she explains. "The kids would meet on the beach and stay together all day, and then they would all come to my house, so we were never really alone."

One day, though, Edna remembers a special time. "We were sitting on the beach, and my hand was under the sand, and his hand was too. I don't know about him," she laughs, "but my hand stayed there so long that it went to sleep. I was not about to move it!"

They dated for six years. "It was awful," reflects Edna. "In those days, people didn't sleep with each other. It was frustrating, and you didn't even know you were frustrated."

The year before they were married, Tod was sent to New York to learn the family business. Although he felt completely unsuited for work in women's specialty shops, he desperately wanted to earn a regular wage so he could get married. He was happy with the $15 a week salary.

Meanwhile, Edna received a fellowship and flew to Mexico where she contracted the dysentery that would plague her for years. Because of her illness, she ended up being gone only for the Fall. Meanwhile, a lonely Tod returned to Boston. Two weeks after Edna returned, and despite the tenuous condition of her health, they got married.

"We both really wanted to get married," she recalls, "and neither of us can remember anybody proposing. It just happened."

And it's been happening for 58 years now.

The Surname Debate

When Edna Hibel married "Tod" Plotkin, she
kept her maiden name professionally. Was she
a women's libber back in the early '40's?
Hardly, but Tod was certainly a liberated man.

When Edna and Tod were first married, Edna's career had already begun. She had sold a number of paintings—all signed "Edna Hibel."

Because the newlyweds felt that "Plotkin," Tod's family name, would be difficult for people to pronounce, they decided Edna should continue to use her maiden name professionally.

After all these years, and having completed thousands of paintings, lithographs, and collectible dolls, Edna now knows they made the right choice. "Hibel is two letters shorter," she laughs, "and I've signed an awful lot of things!"

Tod, on the other hand, says he has never minded when people call him Tod Hibel. He is, after all, the man who decided in the '60s that he would be willing to take over the responsibilities of their house, child rearing and the business end of the galleries, to allow Edna to concentrate on her art. In Tod's mind, it was no big deal, since women gave up their careers and names all the time when they got married.

Perhaps Tod was really the first "Mr. Mom!"

Her Best Review

Some people acknowledged to be giants in their fields seem to love making others feel incompetent, but not Edna Hibel. She is a great believer in not intimidating others just because she has an expertise. She believes that people should be allowed to do what they know best without outside interference, and she practices that philosophy in her everyday life.

When Edna was twenty-three, she decided to give art lessons to her five-year-old cousin. She felt little Ruthie really had talent, but the better Ruthie got, the more trouble she had in school. Evidently, Ruthie's teacher did not like her art, and seemed to constantly find fault with it. Edna decided to discontinue lessons.

"Your teacher knows more than me," she explained to Ruthie. Edna was not about to spoil her little cousin's year.

Later, when Edna's own children started school, she decided that whatever their teachers said about art would be okay with her. She did not want to intimidate them, or in any way nterfere with their way of teaching, even though she was a well-known professional artist.

Edna did, however, agree to help her children's schools whenever she was asked. She once consented to a fund raising painting demonstration. It was so well attended that the school completely funded a scholarship from the proceeds. Edna also gladly accepted an invitation to give a much more intimate demonstration—this one free—to her son Andy's second grade class.

She vividly remembers showing the seven year olds painting techniques as they watched in rapt attention. Her fondest memory of that event, however, was after it ended, when little Andy looked up at her and said, "I was so proud of you, Mommy."

No sold out exhibition could have ever brought her the joy of those few words.

Warm Friends

Everyone knows that Edna Hibel has shared her talent with the world, but sometimes she shares even more than that with her friends. They say she is the type of woman who would give you the shirt off her back. Perhaps that is no exaggeration.

Edna was thrilled when Julian Schwinger, a brilliant theoretical physicist, won the Nobel Prize. She had been childhood friends with his wife, Clarice.

A few days before the Schwingers were to leave for the awards ceremony in Stockholm, Sweden, Clarice asked Edna if she could borrow her fur stole. Clarice explained that her mother and mother-in-law were also going on the trip, but they only had two fur stoles among the three of them. All of Edna's friends knew she had furs, because her father was a furrier.

Edna was happy to send Clarice off in style with the stole. When Clarice called a few days after the event to return the fur, Edna told her to just drop it off at another friend's house.

It was closer to the Schwingers, and Edna knew she would soon be there for a visit.

The next day, Edna's friend asked if she could borrow the mink that Clarice had dropped off. Edna said the one word her friends hear a lot, "Sure!"

In a few days, the friend called to ask if an acquaintance could borrow it. Evidently, the lady was about to go to New York and needed a warm coat. After that, about once a week, Edna would receive a call from some other friend or acquaintance who would ask to borrow the fur. She always said yes.

After the stole had been passed around for months, one of her friends decided there was only one thing to do: throw a party for all the people who had borrowed it. It was a gala

affair, with Edna attending the party in honor of her stole, surrounded by all her furless friends. Of course, the highlight of the evening was when she and the mink were reunited.

The "party animal" had at last come home for a rest. "That mink went to more events in a few months than I had in years!" chuckles Edna.

Grandma's Attic

Located on a street that dead ends into the intercoastal waterway, Edna and Tod's Florida house is spacious, but not pretentious. It is nestled amid overgrown bushes and trees, giving no hint of the treasures that lie inside. From striking original oil paintings, to portfolios of limited edition lithographs, Edna's life work surrounds her, along with beautiful designer vases and unusual gifts presented to her by fans. Family members know that out of sight, there is even more. Fascinating trinkets, early dolls and ceramics, and a variety of cloth, lace, and silk materials have been carefully tucked away, just waiting to be discovered.

Edna Hibel is a pack rat. She has the first drawing she ever did—in fourth grade. It's a reproduction of a magazine cover the teacher told her to draw because she finished her lessons so quickly. She also has the first ceramic figurine she ever did, at age 17, and dolls she made as a young adult.

In fact, her living room is filled with works done at various stages of her career, as well as every gift ever given to her by admiring fans. Vases, intricate pieces of carved ivory, wooden book ends, Mandarin hats acquired on a trip to

China, and a huge number of ceramic figurines are all on display. There is still more piled up in other rooms of the house, and stashed in the attic.

Her daughter in law, Gail, has often found Edna's inability to throw anything away quite convenient. Gail writes and produces murder mystery plays, and has to come up with a lot of costumes for the characters. Once when shopping with her daughter Sami, she couldn't find what she needed for a particular costume. Exasperated, Gail said to Sami, "Let's go to Grandma's attic. We'll find it there."

A customer standing nearby was intrigued. "Where is Grandma's Attic?" she asked. "It sounds like where I should shop." Gail and Sami had to laugh. They knew that not only

was Grandma's attic well stocked, it was the only place in town where everything was free!

Edna's Travels and Exhibitions

Chapter 3

An Afternoon to Remember

Growing up in Boston, Edna became quite an admirer of oriental art. The city has one of the best oriental collections in the country, and Edna spent a great deal of time at the museum pouring over the Asian works. Boston also has an enormous Chinatown, and Edna found many people there willing to pose for her. Some of the oriental people she has captured on canvas will forever remain close to her heart. Other paintings are more memorable for the people who purchased them.

A beautiful painting of a young Chinese woman with her hair pulled up into a bun and wearing a red kimono now hangs in the Hibel Museum in Palm Beach. After the first buyer died, it was resold to someone who later donated it to the museum.

What most people don't realize as they admire the serenely beautiful work, is that whenever Edna looks at it, she thinks of an afternoon trip that was anything but sedate. The man who originally purchased the painting, Mr. Slater, lived in Naples, Florida. A few years after that purchase, Edna found herself in Naples as the guest of honor at a luncheon given by a woman admirer. There at the party sat Mr. Slater, who was delighted to meet his favorite artist. So delighted, in fact, that he insisted that Edna accompany him to his home to see where he was displaying his Hibel masterpiece.

Mr. Slater was so insistent, Edna decided to go. As they approached the Slater house, Edna could see that it was an enormous estate, but when the huge gate swung open she was not prepared for what she saw inside. There were all sorts of exotic animals roaming the grounds—emus, miniature horses, flamingos, and some sort of unusual ducks. Once out of the car, Slater walked Edna straight to the edge of a man-made pond, where a huge manatee poked its nostrils above the surface and contentedly munched some lettuce leaves the host offered him. Then Slater reached down, untied a rope attached to a stake, and pulled a pontoon that was floating in the middle of the pond toward them. He urged Edna to get in, while he remained on shore.

Once she was seated, Slater picked up a life preserver that was tethered to the pontoon and quickly heaved it out into the pond. No sooner had it smacked the surface of the water than a shiny grey dolphin sprang up and grabbed it. Swimming with all its might, the dolphin then raced in circles, pulling the pontoon after it, with a terrified Edna on board.

Fighting the urge to scream, Edna heard Mr. Slater's voice from shore, yelling, "That's Flipper's sister!" Of course, by this time Edna didn't care whose sister was pulling her around—she just wanted it to stop.

Mercifully, the ride ended as abruptly as it had begun, this time with Mr. Slater signaling the dolphin to bring him the life preserver. Once back on land, the artist and her patron ambled across the grounds followed by a honking black seal who slipped into a nearby swimming pool. Edna remembers thinking that after all the excitement, viewing her painting was the least memorable thing about the whole trip.

But now, with that very portrait back at the Hibel Museum, it is obvious that it has come full circle—just as Edna did one strange afternoon in Naples.

Winnie

Edna first met Winnie Cheng at the Boston Museum School of Fine Arts. Winnie told Edna she was the homeliest of five daughters, but Edna thought she was beautiful. So have the thousands of visitors to the Hibel Museum, where her portrait now resides.

When Edna was nineteen, and in her second year of art school, she recruited her friend and fellow art student, a young Chinese woman named Winnie Cheng, to pose for her. Winnie's father had been the right hand man of Sun Yat Sen, head of China's Nationalist Party in the 1920's. Although he was then mayor of Tientsin, his daughter was just one of the many anonymous students at the art school working to perfect her craft. After months of labor, the portrait was completed and sold. Although Edna had done portraits of her friends since she was a little girl, Winnie's was the first to sell.

The two friends became even closer when they both made plans to be married to Harvard graduates. While each young woman looked forward to a loving, happy future, Winnie's plans were more complicated. She and her future husband had decided to return to China to help make it a better place. Winnie felt they could make a difference in the lives of their fellow countrymen.

On Edna's wedding day, Winnie commented, "Oh Edna, I'm so glad the sun is out. In my country they say that if the sun shines on a bride, she'll have a beautiful life." That was the last time Edna saw Winnie before she returned to China.

At first, letters flew from one side of the world to the other regularly, but then Winnie's came less often. Finally, Edna sensed trouble when Winnie sent a letter asking her to send nylons and vitamins. She immediately sent them, concerned that her friend was not able to get such things. Unfortunately, her concerns were well founded. Edna never heard from Winnie again.

As the years went by, the original buyer of Winnie's portrait died and his estate went on auction. Amazingly, a personal friend of Edna's appeared and bought it to donate to the Hibel Museum. The painting had returned, but Edna still missed the friend it portrayed.

Twenty five years later, Edna was in Beijing for an exhibit. With the memory of her lost friend now constantly on her mind, she and Tod decided to try to launch a search for her. They asked every one they met, including members of the media, if they had ever heard of Winnie Cheng, the subject of her portrait.   Wherever they went, the answers were negative.

Back home after her very successful exhibit and very unsuccessful search, she was surprised to receive a letter from a man who introduced himself as Winnie's son. He lived in the United States, but had heard about Edna's search when a relative sent him a Shanghai magazine article about Edna. Once again letters flew across the miles, but this time to the son in America. She learned that Winnie and her husband, who had been university professors, were victims of the 1966-76 Cultural Revolution in China. They had been banished to hard labor in the fields, their dreams of a happy life crushed by cruel misery. After ten or twelve years, they both succumbed to disease and malnutrition.

In 1980, Winnie's son, Henry Cheng, with his own little boy, met Edna in person. Today the correspondence from Henry is posted in the Hibel Museum beside Winnie's beautiful portrait. With the letters are Edna's last gift to her friend— portraits she painted of Winnie's son and grandson, a legacy that managed to escape the tyranny of the country she had so desperately wanted to help.

To Russia, With Love

Hibel paintings have done a lot of traveling. Edna has been invited to exhibit her works in Japan, China, Yugoslavia, Switzerland, Germany, Austria, Costa Rica, England, Finland, Sweden, Norway, Israel, Belgium, Monaco, and Brazil. Luckily, in all Edna's years of traveling, only three of her paintings were ever damaged. There have, however, been some major challenges to overcome when shipping the artwork and setting it up for exhibitions.

When Edna had an exhibit in Russia, her paintings were packed in huge crates and flown first to Helsinki. Unfortunately, after the plane arrived, there was no plane big enough to carry the crates on to St. Petersburg where the show was being held. It was decided that all the paintings would be trucked to the show's location. The trip was uneventful, but once the truck arrived with the artwork, there was quite a problem.

It had taken big forklifts to lift the crates into the truck at the Helsinki airport. At St. Petersburg, however, there was no machinery available. After surveying the situation, the workmen declared that it was impossible to unpack the truck, even though the exhibition opened the next day. Hours went by, but no one could figure out how to remove the crates from the truck.

Finally someone had a bright idea: they could use snow plows to do the job! There was only one small detail—it was June and there were no snow plows around. Hope was fading fast that an art exhibition would take place the next day.

Eventually, it was decided that with careful planning and coordination, the paintings could be uncrated inside the bowels of the truck. It took all day, with Edna glad that she could not understand what the Russian workmen were muttering as they labored, but the paintings were finally removed from their crates and placed on display in the exhibit hall. Edna's worries, however, were far from over.

All day long, through all the discussions and activities, a Russian customs agent sat with a cold expression on his face watching the proceedings. "It looked like he was trying to catch me at something, but I didn't know what," says Edna. As the workmen took the paintings to hang, the agent silently followed them into the building. Edna was concerned, to say the least. "I thought he was going to kill me or something!" she remembers.

Within half an hour, the agent emerged, only this time his face had softened. He approached Edna with a smile, and in perfect English said, "I love your paintings. If there is anything I can do for you, please let me know." Edna's sigh of relief was audible.

Once again, the Hibel paintings had worked their magic. Their silent message of peace and love had parted the iron curtain decades before politicians' rhetoric ever did. Edna Hibel's "speak softly, and carry a big brush" diplomacy seemed to work wonders.

A Hard-Drinking Artist

Edna travels to Europe quite often, most of the time to work at her studio in Zurich. There, the finest quality of materials are available for her to use in collectible plates and her sculpted artwork. She also works with some of the world's master craftsmen there. Although they are never surprised by the exceptional artwork Edna produces, several of them were quite surprised by the artist one night at dinner.

When Edna was in Zurich to sculpt and produced limited edition plates, she met many times with two craftsmen—Mr. Kaiser and Mr. Futterer, who handled the various phases of production. One evening, after their discussions for the day had ended, they invited Edna to dine with them at a very fancy restaurant. Although she was tired, she agreed because she did not want to disappoint them.

The food was elegant and the wine flowed—to everyone but Edna, who has never enjoyed the taste of alcoholic beverages. The men went through one bottle of wine, and then another, continuing to urge Edna to sample some. "They must have asked me ten times if I wanted some wine," she recalls, "but each time I firmly told them no."

Meanwhile, as the men were beginning to enjoy their third bottle, Edna suddenly leaped from her chair, screaming, "Get me some whiskey!!!" The stunned men and the other diners stared in disbelief, while a waiter scrambled to bring her a shot.

"It was a cramp in my leg," she explains, "and I knew just what to do. One teaspoon of whiskey took care of it."

It probably took care of the craftsmen's overindulgence, too. They snapped to attention, turned red, and asked for the check. It was definitely time to end the evening.

Art to Dine For

Edna Hibel's paintings are displayed in museums and universities all over the world, as well as in thousands of private collections. Sometimes even she is surprised by where she finds her artwork.

When Justice Warren Burger invited Edna and Tod to visit the Supreme Court Building in Washington, he took them down to the dining room, where the chief justice is allowed to choose all the artwork. Burger had filled the room with dignified works of art borrowed from the National Gallery, but right in the middle was a bright Hibel reproduction of Geisha girls. "Why did you choose that?" asked a surprised Edna.

Burger replied, "They needed a little something to liven the place up."

Edna didn't care if diners liked the taste of the food, but she certainly hoped they liked the judge's taste in art.

A Very Special Guest

You would think that when Edna Hibel has an art exhibition, she would be the center of attention, but that was not the case at an exhibition in Belgium.

Once Edna and some Hibel Society members traveled to Belgium for an exhibition at a castle in the city of Ghent. As usual, Edna brought her art supplies, never wanting to miss an opportunity to paint.

The day before the show, she went into the countryside to find a subject. After searching for hours, she finally came upon a man plastering high up on a wall surrounded by greenery. She had found her perfect spot. The man indicated that he would be happy to pose for the artist, even donning a huge straw hat that Edna thought would be just the right touch for the scene. Hours later, her painting was done and she gathered up her supplies and waved goodbye to the plasterer. But that was not the last she saw of him.

The exhibition, a formal invitation-only event, opened the next evening. The room was packed. As hundreds of art lovers mingled with Edna and admired her works on display, she had no way of knowing that a certain plasterer had come unannounced to the door. With no invitation and dressed in disheveled work clothes, he was quickly turned away by the guard, who told him that he could only be admitted if he was wearing a tie.

Within the hour he returned, this time in dress clothes. Again the plasterer asked to be admitted, and again the guard turned him away, but this time one of the people who had accompanied Edna on her afternoon painting trip noticed the ongoing drama and signaled that the subject of her painting should be admitted.

As soon as the plasterer came through the door, he began strutting around the room asking people if they would like his autograph. He was perfectly serious. He had decided that the party was in his honor, and he had not wanted to disappoint his guests. "Boy, did he change in one day!" recalls Edna with amusement.

Although the man was the center of attention for hours, Edna did not say a word. After all, she was only the artist, and what is an artist without a subject? She graciously shared the limelight as the celebrity plasterer greeted and entertained his guests. The painting had come to life—and he was the life of the party.

An Alaskan Adventure

There is something about Edna Hibel that endears her to everyone she meets. Is it her ready smile, her genuine interest in others, or her ability to make regular people feel so special? Whatever that indefinable quality, Edna definitely has more than her share.

Edna was very anxious to find Eskimos to paint when she and Tod traveled with the Hibel Society to Alaska, but she couldn't find them anywhere. One day in Seward, Edna decided she might have better luck finding them if she went into the countryside. Unfortunately, there were no taxis to drive them anywhere. In fact, the only transportation they could locate was "Seward's Trolley," a trolley that was strictly designed for in-town trips.

Edna explained her dilemma to the trolley driver, who seemed sympathetic. The driver said that if he didn't get too busy, he would take them. Luckily, only one other woman got on, and she too wanted a long ride with her kids, so they were off on their adventure.

Hours went by, with no sign of Eskimos, but the trip itself was a joy. The trolley driver seemed thrilled to be entertaining an artist, and went out of his way to show Edna and Tod a good time. They chatted constantly, and the driver even insisted on taking Edna's photograph.

The driver stopped at one point and called ahead to a neighboring town to try to find out if there were any Eskimos around. Finally, he located one beautiful Eskimo mother and her child. Edna quickly sketched them.

While the search continued for more Eskimos, the driver told Edna all about the beat up old conductor's hat he was wearing. "This belonged to my father and my grandfather before him," he said proudly. "My grandfather worked on the first Alaska railroad."

Finally, the driver delivered them to the ship just before it was to leave. As the ship pulled out of the harbor, Edna was told that a package had been delivered for her. Carefully unwrapping the mysterious box, she found inside the conductor's hat and a note from the driver telling her how much he enjoyed meeting her.

The treasured hat is now on display in the Hibel Museum. Little had Edna known that while she and Tod were searching for Eskimos, the trolley driver must have been searching for artists.

A Friendly Hug

Edna does not think of herself as any more considerate than most people, but those who know her say she is exceptionally thoughtful. However, even those closest to her might be surprised by the lengths to which she has gone to keep someone from feeling badly.

When Edna began making limited edition plates in the 1970s, she often went to Europe and worked closely with a number of craftsmen in the area. One of the most talented, as well as one of the most unusual, was Wilhelm Heublein.

Edna describes Wilhelm as a short, but very strong man. Whenever he would come into her workshop in Zurich, he would grab Edna and hug her until she hurt all over. She says he also kissed everyone so hard on their cheeks that they had sore faces when he finished! Edna knew he meant no harm. He was just very enthusiastic and friendly—but on one occasion, Heublein's exuberance actually caused her quite a bit of pain.

Edna and Tod had gone to Vienna to prepare for one of her exhibitions. Members of the Hibel Society were there, too, and huge crowds were anticipated. The day before the opening, Heublein arrived in town, and wasted no time in coming to see his favorite artist.

When Edna was told that he was waiting for her in the hotel lobby, she ran down the stairs to meet him. "As usual," she related, "he grabbed me, but this time he also lifted me up and squeezed me really tight." Two friends standing beside her heard a crack, and one even commented that it sounded as though he had broken her ribs. Indeed he had, and Edna immediately experienced a searing pain. Amazingly, she carried on as though nothing had happened, and never even told Wilhelm what he had done.

"He would have felt terrible," she explained, "so I didn't want him to know." Besides, Edna was not about to disappoint her admirers. With her exhibition opening the next day, the Hibel Society members had already arrived to cheer her on, and all the events and meals were planned around her. She remembers thinking, "The show must go on!"

She suffered in silence for three days, not even telling Tod until the festivities were concluded. She wasn't about to let a few broken bones spoil an event, or a friendship.

Only the Best for the Guest

Besides being a talented German craftsman, Wilhelm Heublein also tried his hand at producing wine. He had a small vineyard behind his house that produced about a thousand bottles of wine a year, most of which, according to Edna, he drank himself.

Although Edna worked closely with Wilhelm for years, she had never met his wife. Finally, Wilhelm convinced Edna to come to his home for dinner. Evidently his wife was a Hibel admirer who wanted very much to meet the artist in person, even though she could speak little English.

After a fabulous meal, Mrs. Heublein abruptly jumped up from the table, and without saying a word in German or English, ran down to their wine cellar. She returned with two interesting looking bottles of wine, which she eagerly held out to Edna.

The color seemed to drain from Wilhelm's face. "You're going to give her those?" he blurted out. Mrs. Heublein simply nodded her head, as she presented the gift to Edna. Wilhelm was speechless.

Later Edna discovered the reason for Wilhelm's reluctance. People everywhere wanted to buy that particular wine. It had the reputation of being the best wine in the country, but it was not for sale. The neighbor who produced the wine refused offers to sell his treasure, preferring instead to consume it himself, or give it away to good friends.

Evidently, Wilhelm was not friends with the family, so he was thrilled beyond belief to have somehow gotten his hands on it. For months, he had relished the thought of consuming it himself, just waiting for a special occasion to uncork it. Of course, now that day would never come. His wife had given it to an artist who didn't even drink!

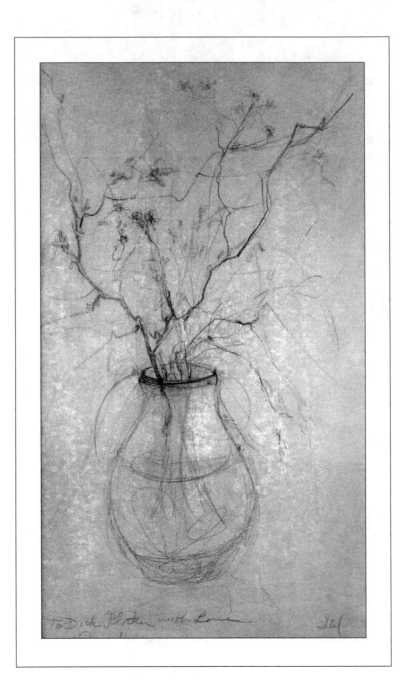

to Dick Ploter with Love

Mixed Media

Chapter 4

Watercolors

Most people think of Edna Hibel's paintings as oils on canvas. Actually, she has also done a lot of watercolors. She usually works outside, with her paper flat on the ground so the paints won't run. Sometimes, though, she has found herself running.

Edna loves watercolors, and did a lot of them in her youth. In fact, one summer when she was a teenager, she received a scholarship to study with Eliot O'Hara, a famous watercolorist. Edna recalls that O'Hara used to say, "It takes two people to do a watercolor, one to do the painting and one to hit the artist over the head when he should stop."

That summer O'Hara also seemed to think it took two artists whenever he was called on for certain demonstrations. If he had to produce scenes with people in them, he would ask Edna to come up and draw their figures and faces. He was much more adept at doing landscapes, and knew that Edna did people very well—especially their faces. "I ask you to do the people because you're so much better at it than I am," he explained. "With your talent and my knowledge, we would be a genius if we were one person!"

One day when Edna and Eliot were outside painting, she found out he really meant what he said. The clouds had begun to darken and suddenly it started to sprinkle. O'Hara immediately leaped up from his bench, grabbed Edna's painting, and jumped into the car, leaving his own painting in the rain. "Hurry up!" he yelled to Edna, "Grab my stuff and get into the car!"

A puzzled Edna began to gather up all the supplies, including O'Hara's artwork, but despite her efforts, the heavens opened up and everything was drenched. As she climbed into the car with O'Hara's ruined painting, she asked why he had taken her painting and not his own. "Yours was better," was his only explanation.

That was enough for Edna. She still treasures her painting from that day—drops and all.

A Fish Story

When asked about the most unusual thing she ever painted, Edna Hibel commented, "Nothing is unusual, and everything is unusual. Just to be able to do them makes them all wonderful." Still, on reflection, Edna does remember one quite unique painting situation.

When Edna was in Maine doing watercolors, she stopped at a pond and began to paint the scene. She had noticed that there were big trout-like fish in the water, but didn't think much about painting them until a stranger came along who said the pond was his. When Edna mentioned that the fish were beautiful, the man replied, "Would you like them to pose for you?"

With that, the man dipped his hand into the water. Within a few seconds, one of the fish swam into his palm. He quickly lifted it out of the water and held it until he could tell it was in distress. Then he replaced the desperate creature and plucked another one out to pose. The routine continued until all the fish had posed at least once and Edna had completed the painting. "Thank goodness watercolors are quick!" she reflects.

Edna will never forget the day she painted those flopping fish. Someday she may paint subjects more unusual than those she did that day, but it's doubtful that she will ever paint any who are more anxious for her to finish.

The patient fish can be seen posing at the Hibel Museum whenever Edna's watercolor works are featured.

Edna Does Dishes

Some art lovers think that Edna Hibel is an artist who does just oil paintings, whereas others think she does just lithographs, or just dolls. Still others think of her as the artist who does only limited edition collector plates. Edna is amused by all the misconceptions, because the truth is that she is a very versatile artist, working in a wide variety of materials and mediums, but that was not always the case.

Producing limited edition collector plates was not Edna Hibel's idea. In fact, she had never considered such a thing. Her first collector plate, done in 1973, came about because a Royal Doulton representative for the United States saw one of her mother-daughter lithographs and fell in love with it. It took him a while to locate the artist, but he finally succeeded.

Edna and Tod were surprised when they got a call from a Mr. Polk, who asked if she had ever considered working in porcelain plates. Despite Tod explaining that, "We don't know anything about dishes," Mr. Polk asked their permission to take a painting back to England and have it reproduced on a plate. They only agreed because they felt there was nothing to lose.

Edna loved the translucent quality of porcelain when she saw the completed sample. "That's what I've been trying to do in oils when I layer one color over another," she told Tod. They both thought that the plate was beautiful. Then, despite being warned that the collector plate industry was dying, Edna decided to go ahead and produce a series of six mother-daughter plates. Each plate was an immediate and resounding success. So much so, that the first of that series, *Collette and Child*, is displayed in a Chicago plate museum as "The Plate that Saved the Collector Plate Industry." To Edna, it was just something new and exciting to do in her ever-expanding repertoire.

A Masterpiece Returns

Over the years, Edna Hibel has created beautiful limited edition dolls done in wax, porcelain and wood, fashionably dressed in lace and beaded gowns, but the first dolls she produced were not the finely crafted collector dolls she is known for today.

When she was in elementary school, Edna began making dolls not because she liked to play with them, but because she liked to sew. She would spend hours taking scraps of material and attaching them to inexpensive plastic doll heads which her mother would buy. Then she would carefully stuff the little bodies with cotton and sew them closed. For some of the dolls, the finishing touch would come when she would cut off a swatch of her own hair and attach it to the doll's head. She was much more concerned with their hair than her own!

Edna noticed that sometimes, after making a doll, it would seem to disappear. Years later, she discovered that her mother had been giving them away to her friends. Most of the time, the missing dolls never really bothered Edna, because by the time she realized one doll was gone, she would already be hard at work creating another one.

But there was one doll that she missed a lot. She had made it when she was only eight, and in Edna's mind, it was exquisite. Over the years, the doll lingered in her memory as one of the most finely crafted babies she had ever produced. She remembered the carefully sewn flowered dress that matched the pillow and bedding on its "bed"—a converted matchbox. She often thought of that doll when she worked on a new collector doll, trying to make it as beautiful as she remembered that one from her childhood.

When an old friend announced that she had saved that very doll for fifty years, and was now donating it to the Hibel Museum, Edna eagerly awaited its arrival. She had a rude awakening when she discovered a four inch simply sewn childish rendition of a doll with a smashed in little plastic head. "This is it?" she remembers thinking, "It looks like something a child would make."

Even so, Edna does not plan to part with it again. It is kept not at the museum, but at home with other dolls she created in her youth. They may be dressed in simple cotton and have cost only pennies to make, but they were the inspirations that paved the way for the popular designer dolls she now sells for thousands of dollars each.

Film Artist

For years, Tod and Edna talked of having a movie made about their travels and love of life in general. It was their friend Ginger Rogers who finally convinced them to stop talking and actually make the film themselves.

A trip Edna and Tod had planned to Europe seemed like a perfect movie-making opportunity. They decided not only to do the movie, but also to invite their son Jon and his wife Gail to meet them there for the big adventure. Little did Jon know how much of the adventure would ultimately depend on him.

Edna and Tod wanted everything to be perfect for the couple, because this was their first trip to Europe. The plan was to meet them in Venice and make the movie there. Eager to start, Tod purchased a huge movie camera and started testing it out while awaiting their arrival. Unfortunately, before Jon and Gail arrived, the big camera proved to be a mistake—Tod severely injured his back trying to carry it around. He was miserable and bedridden, but he wasn't about to spoil the trip for everybody. At Tod's insistence, Edna went ahead and made reservations at an elegant palace, so at least the two couples would be in wonderful surroundings, but even that idea didn't work out. No sooner had Jon and Gail arrived than the hotel workers went on strike and the visions of elegant service never materialized. The trip seemed doomed.

Despite all the problems, the family decided the show must go on. First, Edna rented a car with a seat that would go all the way down on the passenger side so that Tod, still unable to even sit up, could accompany them on their film making trip.

Then Tod appointed Jon, who had never handled a movie camera in his life, to succeed him as cameraman. Jon had to learn to be a film maker fast. Somehow, Tod managed to demonstrate how to use the camera while flat on his back, because they ended up getting some exceptional footage. It was probably the first time in the history of film making that a movie was directed by someone who could not even see what was being filmed. Tod's vantage point was below the car's window.

Although "The World I Love," narrated by the artist, has never been formally released, it has been shown many times at the Hibel Museum and at galleries throughout the United States that have requested it. It depicts the people Edna loves to paint, such as women working in the fields and children with their mothers. It also has beautiful scenes from Venice, the hills of Switzerland, and the Zurich workshop where Edna produces her lithographs.

The only thing missing from the film was its director, but Tod would probably rather forget where he was during the film's production. He says directing left him kind of flat.

The Cameramen's Surprise

Despite the family's successful filming of "The World I Love," Edna decided that she should have professionals do a film featuring her lithography techniques. However, she didn't count on the professionals' reactions to her art.

Once, Edna agreed to be featured in a film about how to make lithographs. The crew of film makers arrived at her summer home right about lunch time, and were greeted by Gail, Edna's daughter-in-law. Because of the hour, Gail insisted that they sit down for lunch before any work began.

After some preliminary pleasantries, discussions began over how to start the film. The man in charge asked Edna what she was presently working on. When she explained that she was doing a painting of Gail, he quickly replied, "Then that's what we'll start filming." Both Gail and Edna thought that would be fine.

After the meal, everyone proceeded to Edna's studio where she began her work. Almost immediately, the men's jaws dropped open and their faces turned bright red. Without warning, Gail had whisked off her clothes and had begun posing.

"Gail and I didn't know what to do. We thought, 'what's so horrible about this?' They wanted me to continue what I was working on," explains Edna, adding, "Gail was always one of my best nude models. She can get undressed in a second!"

Affordable Art

Like other famous artists, Edna Hibel's original paintings sell for thousands of dollars, but one thing that sets Edna Hibel apart from other artists is that she also loves to produce art inexpensive enough for admirers who don't have big pocketbooks.

"I always liked the idea that people can own something with my image when they can't afford originals," she says. In fact, Edna was delighted when she began producing inexpensive items such as decorated note paper, wooden boxes with enamel images, scarves, etc. for the Edna Hibel Museum shop.

The truth of the matter is, Edna and Tod were not thinking about sales when the museum first opened. They were just thrilled to have a permanent repository for her art. "When the museum opened, we didn't know that we should have a shop," she recalls, "but visitors kept wanting to buy something, so we decided to produce some less expensive items." Now guests love choosing something to take home to remember the museum experience.

Edna also loved learning to make lithographs. "There's nothing wrong with owning copies," she contends. "I really enjoy making them and showing people how they are produced." Once Edna had groups of Hibel Society members come to her workshop to observe her creating images on stone faces and "pulling" lithographs. She worked tirelessly all day, much to the delight of those who were fascinated watching the many steps involved in the process. They were impressed with the exacting standards for the copies, and were thrilled when they were presented with the lithographs they had watched her complete that day.

"One small group after another would be brought into the workshop," Edna explains. "It had to be carefully planned, because no one would be able to see me working if the whole group had come at once. Then, at the end of the day, we wanted to be sure to give each group copies of the lithograph it had seen being done. It was quite a production."

With her inexhaustible energy and her enthusiasm about everything she creates, perhaps the only thing that can't be copied is the artist herself. Edna Hibel is truly an original.

Adventures with the Rich and Famous

Chapter 5

You Be the Judge

Edna Hibel always looks for the good in everyone she meets. She takes people at face value, as human beings with innate dignity, whether they labor in the fields or have advanced degrees. For that reason, she rarely asks people what they do for a living. But one time, quite unexpectedly, she found herself doing just that, and the exchange that followed is one she will never forget.

One day Tod and Edna visited their Palm Beach museum on their way to run some errands. Lena, who was then running the museum, greeted Edna with the news that there was a lovely couple who had just purchased a painting and would love to meet her. After a brief introduction, when Edna did not really catch the couple's name, they started chatting. Although it was out of character for Edna, she asked what the man did for a living. He answered simply, "I do judging." Edna recalls thinking, "Judging—maybe beauty contests or cows, or something."

Just then, a photographer friend opened the gallery door, waved to Edna, and quickly retreated. Because Edna always wanted to help her friends with their businesses, she announced to the couple that the person they had just seen was a very eminent photographer. "Oh," said the man, "What type of photographs does he take?"

"He does documentaries," Edna explained. "He just did one called the Titticut Follies, which takes place in an insane asylum."

At that, the nice gentleman looked surprised and said, "I don't think they can show that publicly."

Edna vehemently disagreed, saying, "Oh yes they can. It's wonderful! Of course they can."

About that time, she noticed Tod standing in the distance wildly waving his hands to get her attention. "How strange," she thought as she continued the discussion. "It's a wonderful movie."

Again the man insisted, "But I don't think it can be shown."

"No, you're wrong!" Edna stated matter-of-factly, as Tod moved closer to her side.

"Edna, This is Chief Justice Warren Burger of the Supreme Court," he explained, "and that movie is up before the Court because they are trying to stop it from being shown."

"Oh, so that's what you judge!" exclaimed a shocked Edna. She was supremely embarrassed.

The First Hibelite

Fame and Fortune have come to Edna Hibel, but they have never defined her life, as Ginger Rogers once discovered.

In 1963, a glamorous Ginger Rogers was appearing in Boston at a theater-in-the-round. Whenever she was photographed, she looked glowingly happy, but the truth was that Ginger's appearance was a facade. Emotionally, she was a wreck. Because she was a Christian Scientist, she made an appointment to see the head of the Christian Science Church, Mr. Craig, to seek his counsel. At their first meeting, she explained to Craig that she was miserable in what was her fifth attempt at marriage, and stated that for all her fame and fortune, what she really wanted in life was a happy marriage.

Craig responded by taking her to meet the two people whom he felt had the happiest marriage in the world. That very evening, Ginger found herself at Edna and Tod's house for dinner. They all spent a wonderful evening together, and Ginger witnessed a loving relationship beyond anything she had ever imagined.

About two years later, Ginger came back to Boston to play the leading role in "Hello Dolly." At that point, she commissioned Edna to do her portrait, and let the artist decide what she should wear. Edna decided to paint Ginger in her stage costume. It was a bright red dress made of heavy drapery material the star had chosen herself. The look was completed with a yellow wig and a huge hat with a plume. While posing, Edna learned that Ginger was miserable in the costume under the stage lights, because it was so hot, but you would never know it from seeing the finished work.

With Ginger posing for innumerable sessions, she and Edna became very good friends. In fact, when the theater run had ended, and Edna needed to take some new paintings to her New York gallery, the star asked if they could make the trip together. Although Ginger had a fancy limousine at her disposal, she traveled with Edna and Tod in their station wagon because she said it made her happy to be around them.

It must have been a strange site, three adults squeezed into a station wagon's front seat, with a limousine traveling behind them—filled to the brim with fancy luggage. When Edna kidded Ginger about having so many suitcases, she explained that any time the press took a picture of her, she felt she had to give away whatever clothes she was wearing. It was hard for Edna to empathize, since she had never cared at all about clothes.

During the trip, whenever they stopped for a bathroom break, Ginger would put on a huge hat, tie it around her neck with a scarf and don her darkest sunglasses, hoping she would not be recognized. Because she seemed quite pleased with her disguise, Edna did not have the heart to tell her what she overhead two "old biddies" say as they came strolling out of the ladies room where Ginger was freshening up. One whispered to the other, "Who in the world does she think she is? Ginger Rogers or something?"

After a few years, Ginger heard that some of Edna's admirers were thinking about starting a fan club, and she insisted on becoming the first paying member. Her $10 check for the Hibel Society, however, was never cashed. Tod paid the fee himself and framed Ginger's check. He wanted to commemorate the first "Hibelite."

On reflecting on her friend's lifetime of failed marriages, Edna recalls that Ginger would often say, "If only I could meet a Tod," but unfortunately, she continued to choose men who were very different from Tod. Sadly, she passed away in 1995, still looking for her Tod.

After Rogers' death, her portrait was returned to Edna for the Hibel Museum. It is an enormous work, showing a happy, glamorous actress at the height of her popularity. It's how Ginger would want her fans to remember her.

The Royal Line

Anyone who meets Edna Hibel is struck by her down-to-earth manner. There is no sense of superiority or pretense. She seems comfortable and real, and makes you feel comfortable in turn. It is difficult to imagine such an unassuming person hobnobbing with celebrities and royalty, but the interesting thing about Edna is she loves all people—even rich and famous ones.

Some years ago, Queen Elizabeth marked the 25th anniversary of her reign by having a very big celebration. In fact, it was the greatest convention of royalty in European history. "King and Queen of this, Prince of that, every country you could think of was represented," remembers Edna.

She and Tod were invited to participate in three days of the festivities because Edna had donated the proceeds from her London exhibition to the Order of St. John, the English equivalent of our Red Cross. The Queen heads up the charity, and was very grateful for Hibel's contribution.

"We were put up at the Ritz, and all we had to do was to be downstairs at certain times so that a limousine could take us to the different affairs," says Edna. They had lunch at the House of Lords, attended an affair at St. James Palace, and participated in other activities at various famous churches.

Many times they found themselves sharing their limousine with another couple. "They were just darling," reports Edna. "We became very friendly, but we didn't catch their names." The gentleman kept saying Edna should come to Paris and paint him. Edna and Tod would just laugh, not taking him seriously.

The days passed quickly, and it was soon time for what was to be the culmination of the celebration—a banquet where Edna and Tod were to be presented to Queen Elizabeth and about 30 other royals in attendance.

The big moment finally came, and Tod and Edna began to be presented by one member of royalty to a reception line of other royals. As they proceeded down the long line of kings and queens, they suddenly found themselves face-to-face with their friends from the limo. It turned out that he was Prince d' Polignac of Paris, cousin of Prince Rainier of Monaco. "If there was a throne in France, he would be second in line to it," explains Edna.

Instead of the usual pleasantries being exchanged during that presentation, Tod and Edna found themselves being invited to lunch—at the Palace of Versailles no less! Then the Prince asked if they knew where it was.

"We'll find it," replied Edna as she stifled a giggle.

Weeks later, Tod and Edna found themselves at Versailles Palace. "The place was just jammed," recalls Tod. "And there he was," continues Edna, "with his plumes and every-thing." He was being honored because he was retiring as the head of the Knights of Malta. As with others they had met, Tod and Edna soon became very good friends, and visited the d' Polignacs whenever they were in Paris.

More recently, the Prince and Princess came to America, and invited Edna and Tod to a big party given for them at a Palm Beach mansion. "The only people we knew there were the caterers!" Edna says laughing.

An Unfulfilled Dream

You would think that a world famous artist like Edna Hibel would have realized her every dream, but as she found out, you don't always get what you want.

In 1939, a seventeen-year-old Edna won a year's scholarship to study in Europe. When she won the trip, she dreamed of going to Paris and meeting Picasso, whom she greatly admired.

"I planned to go knock on his door, and ask him to give me lessons," she recalls. If he refused, Edna was prepared to rent an apartment as near to his as possible, so she could keep trying to convince him, but her big adventure never materialized. She ended up going to Mexico instead, because war was already breaking out in Europe.

Reflecting on her youthful exuberance, Edna now realizes, "Maybe it's better I didn't get to go to Paris. At the time I didn't know Picasso was such a dirty old man."

The Important Things in Life

Chapter 6

The Magic of Mothers and Babies

Every Edna Hibel art lover knows that mother-child themes are common in her art. Even as a child, she loved playing with young children and filled notebooks with sketches of babies, but she had not yet discovered her signature mother-child portraits. That particular theme did not occur to her until she went to Mexico as a young adult.

Edna Hibel dearly loves mothers and babies. She feels that the mother-infant relationship is actually what makes us all part of the human race. "I've found that there is something between the mother and baby that to me means living," Edna explains. "You can go to any country, and you see that the clothes are different, the language is different, and they carry the babies differently, but the look between the mother and the baby is exactly the same."

What Edna sees in mothers and their infants is a wonderful pulling together that she describes as "exquisite." The look in the infant's eyes seems to say, "I know you will do for me what you can do, and I will give you pleasure that no one else could give you."

Although she is not sure which mother-infant painting was her first, she does remember that she first thought of the theme in Mexico, where she went right after art school in 1939. One particular scene she vividly remembers was when she was painting a woman who was ironing clothes. Every hour or two the woman's daughter, who was only about eight, would bring in her baby sister to nurse. The three made fantastic subjects for the young Edna.

"When infants look into their mothers' eyes, it is like their souls are meeting," explains Edna. "There is nothing else like it, and that's what I try to capture in my paintings."

In Edna's ideal world, mothers accept their parenting duties with joy, and radiate an inner peace which their children reflect. Art lovers everywhere, male and female, seem to appreciate the sentiment of those paintings and want to capture it for themselves. When asked if she herself personified the serene mother when her children were infants, Edna replies emphatically, "No! It seems to me I was always busy trying to do so many things at once."

As pressured as any young mother trying to balance a career and motherhood, Edna was simply a busy woman who had the sensitivity to notice the magical spark between infants and their mothers, and then took the time to capture what we all long to enjoy for a lifetime. It doesn't take a serene mother to do that—just a talented one with a vision of a better world.

A Celebrity Servant

Edna Hibel treats everyone she meets with respect, even if someone does not treat her respectfully. Also, because of her refined sense of empathy for others, she would never embarrass people by pointing out mistakes they have made. She simply smiles when she recalls one tourist's mistaken notion about her.

Count Bernadotte, a wealthy German aristocrat who was a great admirer of Edna's art, once gave her a number of green aprons to wear while she painted in preparation for the opening of her exhibit at his castle. While working one day in her apron, she realized that she needed to run from the studio to her hotel room nearby to gather some materials. In her haste, she left her apron on. Never one to lose valuable painting time, she began to race up the hotel steps to her room, but she was stopped dead in her tracks. There at the bottom of the steps stood an imposing woman who wore a furious expression.

"Miss!" she bellowed, "Will you *PLEASE* get me a taxi?" It was only then that Edna realized that everyone on the staff at the hotel wore green aprons. Never one to disappoint,

she bowed meekly, stammering, "Right away, Madam," and
ran to tell the hotel staff to call a taxi. Then she sneaked out
the back door.

A Graduation to Remember

Traditionally, graduation ceremonies are exciting occasions, but not because of the speakers. Their messages are usually forgotten more quickly than they would like to admit. But when Edna Hibel was invited to speak at a commencement, the students were in for a treat.

About five years ago, Edna was invited to give the commencement address at Eureka College in Illinois, where she was to receive an honorary degree. Her first thought was, "How can I compete with these people who give speeches all the time, like professors and all the others with such marvelous brains?" She and Tod talked a lot about what she could say, and she put her thoughts on paper, but she was still uneasy as the date approached.

A few hours before the commencement ceremony, the president of the college had a luncheon for the honored guests. Mr. Burg, the Hibel Society President, was also there.

"You really should see Edna give a demonstration," he commented to the college president, who replied that he would love to.

Edna's pulse started racing. "Really?" she asked. "Do you mean that?" When he answered in the affirmative, Edna told him she just happened to have her paints with her. "If you don't mind," she said, "I'd love to do a painting for my speech." Edna was relieved when the president agreed, because she was always relaxed in front of a crowd when she had a paintbrush in her hand.

One lucky student was quickly chosen to pose for the artist, and an easel and art supplies were strategically placed near the traditional lectern. Finally, it was Edna's turn to speak. As she picked up her brush, she told the students, "This big empty canvas is just what your life is now. You can do anything you want to with it." Then she began painting, talking about various decisions she had to make to complete the project, just as they would have many decisions to make along their own life paths. Her major point was that each student would be the one to make the decisions to determine how his or her life turned out. "You're the boss!" she concluded.

After the unique commencement address, the impressed president of the college remarked that the students would certainly remember her speech. But the best review came from one of the professors, who remarked, "You know, I didn't see one kid fall asleep!"

Exhausted but exhilarated, Edna herself was ready for a nap.

A Matter of Appearances

Edna Hibel has never been a "showy" person. Despite being surrounded by her own beautiful works of art, neither she nor Tod have ever paid much attention to appearances. In fact, she rarely plans what to wear ahead of time—it's just not important to her. To this day she cannot remember what she wore when she was presented to the Queen of England, so it should not be surprising that she is rarely the best dressed woman at her own exhibitions.

One day a woman dropped in unexpectedly at Edna's house. Knowing she looked a wreck, Edna apologized for her appearance. Then, on consideration, she blurted out, "But I never look much better than this!" Later that year, she ran into the same woman at one of her exhibitions. Edna was mortified. She was wearing a dress three sizes too big. "Well," thought Edna, "I guess she knows I was telling the truth that day."

Edna had stopped in to see her mother at one of the Hibel galleries on her way to the show. Lena had insisted she change into an extra dress that happened to be there because the one Edna had been wearing was stained.

Still today, Edna does not take fashion seriously, and rarely shops for clothes. She has always preferred to wear the clothes already hanging in her closet rather than buy anything new. Although there have been numerous occasions over the years when Edna vaguely remembers being underdressed or dressed more comfortably than fashionably, she is rarely self conscious. She is much too interested in meeting new people and greeting old friends wherever she goes to think about what she is wearing.

Edna does, however, recall a time when her clothes were acceptable, but she needed to focus a little more carefully on her overall appearance. It was when she had a big exhibition planned at Cape Cod. She went swimming right before the opening, and then hastily jumped into her clothes and went to the event.

Soon guests crowded in and began telling Edna how wonderful she was, but her mother, Lena, was aghast when she arrived. "Look at your hair!" she shouted. Then, while Edna continued to shake the admirers' hands, Lena pulled out a hairbrush and proceeded to brush her daughter's hair right there in the reception line.

"It's hard to feel important when your mother is standing there brushing your hair," reflects Edna.

Actually, the artist has always done quite well with one type of brush—the painting kind.

Mutual Admiration

The people we admire the most are those who exemplify how we want to be. Although Edna Hibel's favorite artist is a Renaissance master, Piero della Francesca, she would not choose any artist as the person she most admires. Surprisingly, the person in history who Edna would most like to emulate has never been associated with the art world at all.

Edna does not believe in past lives, but says if she was the reincarnation of someone, she would want that person to be Lincoln. "I've always admired him because he cared so much about people, and he tried to do his best for the country. I've read about the letters he used to send to mothers and wives whose loved ones had been killed at war. He didn't have to do that. He seemed like a wonderful person."

At 5' 2" tall, Edna hardly resembles her hero physically, but those who know her philosophy can see quite a resemblance. She demonstrates empathy and respect for everyone she encounters, and sees the dignity in her fellow man—whether they are field workers or heads of state. Her art has been characterized as exemplifying a true democratic society, in which all individuals can reach their full potential and live lives of excellence, grace and beauty in harmony with their fellow citizens.

Lincoln would be quite a fan.

Edna's Ethics

Although Edna loves to grant friends' requests, there are a few things that she just won't do, as Chief Justice Warren Burger of the United States Supreme Court found out.

Justice Warren Burger and Edna Hibel became good friends after the Burgers purchased a number of her paintings. Once, he asked Edna and Tod to stop by when they were going through Washington, so he could show them the Supreme Court. They decided to take him up on his offer.

When they arrived, the first thing they noticed in the Justice's chambers was a huge painting, a profile, that someone had done of him. "Could you fix this?" Burger asked Edna as he pointed to the face, "I don't like the nose."

Edna was shocked, and immediately declined, explaining that it would be wrong to touch someone else's painting. "Well," said Burger, "Either you do it, or I'll do it myself."

Some months later, he reported to Edna that he had indeed changed the nose himself. "I never asked how he did it," Hibel recalled, "but better him than me."

An Artist's Self-Portrait

At 81 years old, Edna Hibel has a lot to brag about. After all, she was the youngest artist to ever have a work selected for a major American museum. She has been awarded two honorary doctorates. She has received the Medal of Honor and a Citation from Pope John Paul II. She has had her artwork selected for a United Nations Postage Stamp. She was the founder of the Boston Art Festival. She has had exhibitions all over the world, has a fan club of thousands, and much, much more. Amazingly, despite an incredible list of accomplishments, she is a very modest celebrity.

Those who know Edna say that she is, today, the way she always was—generous and considerate, looking for the good in everyone she meets. The truth of the matter is that Edna, the renowned artist, doesn't see herself as anything special.

"Nobody knows everything about everything—including me. That's what would make someone really special," she explains. "I don't think there are more than a handful of people who ever lived who should be considered special."

To Edna, that handful would include people like Einstein and Leonardo da Vinci, although she admits that even they probably did not know everything about everything.

Because she doesn't see herself as special, she is amused when fans act otherwise, such as when an admirer once recognized her in the Hibel Museum. Edna remembers that the tourist's face turned red and she started to sweat. Then she stammered out, "Well you're just an ordinary person, like me!"

"I wonder what she thought I was?" laughs Edna.

She has also been amused when fans spot her and then run around trying to find a phone so they can call their relatives and friends to tell them who they just saw. "It's not like I'm a celebrity," she states matter-of-factly.

She patiently obliges when admirers in art stores ask her to show them exactly what brushes and paints she buys, convinced that her talent will rub off. "It happens a lot," Edna confesses.

Once, someone admiring a Hibel painting on display at one of her galleries was shocked to suddenly see the artist standing nearby. "You're not dead yet!" the woman blurted out.

Another time she was doing a painting demonstration on a cruise ship when one of those watching shouted, "You're not holding the brush right. My teacher says you're supposed to hold it like this!" and proceeded to demonstrate "the proper technique" to the surprised crowd.

No matter what they ask, or how outrageous their actions, Edna just smiles and treats everyone with respect. After all, she is just a fellow human being—nothing special.

In Search of Beauty

Edna Hibel is one of America's most beloved and versatile artists. People flock to her exhibitions all over the world and love to shop at her galleries. Since 1994, thousands have joined the Edna Hibel Society, and loyally travel to her many exhibitions just to support her efforts. Meanwhile, sales of her oil paintings, serigraphs, collector plates, dolls, porcelain and bronze figurines and other works continue to be very impressive. In fact, she is considered the most successful female artist in the world. Why are people so attracted to her art?

When asked why people love her work, Edna replies, "Maybe it's because I love people so much. I try to express the love I feel for people."

She remembers a 1965 London exhibition when a reporter asked her what she was trying to express in her paintings. She replied, "I feel like I'm on a soapbox yelling, 'You should love!'"

The next day, the reporter's story characterized Edna as a "Hippie Grandmother". "I think she confused me with the flower children of the time," Edna laughs.

Tod tries to explain the popularity of his wife's art by saying, "Edna has an exquisite sense of what is beautiful. She is very sensitive to beauty. What she's doing when she is painting is searching for beauty, and everybody, every day, is searching for beauty. They just don't realize it."

"It's funny, they really don't, do they?" adds Edna.

Her patrons may not know they are searching for beauty, but judging from the sales of her art, they must know when they find it.

Edna Hibel

Biography

Edna Hibel has been painting for more than seven decades. She is considered the most successful woman painting in the United States today, with her style compared to that of Italian Renaissance artist Leonardo da Vinci and the American impressionist Mary Cassatt.

She completed her training at the Boston Museum School of Fine Arts in 1939 and was awarded the prestigious Ruth B. Sturtevant Traveling Fellowship for a year of study and painting in Mexico.

In 1940, she became the youngest artist to have one of her paintings purchased for the permanent collection at the Boston Museum of Fine Art. She returned to the Boston Museum School later for graduate study in the art and techniques of the Renaissance.

While many admirers know her for sensitive portrayals of mothers and children from all cultures, her subject matter also includes flowers, individual portraits, landscapes, and animals. Besides original oil paintings, Hibel has created watercolors, porcelain collector plates, limited edition dolls, lithographs, serigraphs, porcelain and bronze figurines, and a variety of affordable objects such as music boxes, scarves, gift boxes, jewelry, etc.

Hibel has received four honorary doctorates and innumerable other tributes and awards for her art and her humanitarian acts throughout the world. Major museums and galleries in twenty countries on four continents have held exhibitions of her work, and her paintings are in the collections of many of America's universities, public museums, and private collections. Hibel Museum of Art is the world's only non-profit, public museum dedicated to the art of a living American artist.

In November 2001, she was awarded the prestigious Leonardo da Vinci World Award of Arts, the second American (the first being Robert Rauschenberg) and only the second woman to ever receive the honor.

Her "fan club," the Edna Hibel Society, currently has over 3,000 members who enjoy following the artist all over the world for her exhibitions and demonstrations. They also love hearing her real-life stories, which are the subject of this book.

Hibel has been married to Theodore "Tod" Plotkin since 1940, and has three sons and five grandchildren.

Humanitarian and Civic Awards, Honors and Tributes

2003   Completion and Presentation of 600th Hibel Lithograph, "The Epic"

2003   (Jan 17) Dedication Ceremony of Edna Hibel Fine Arts Complex, and Grand Opening of Hibel Museum of Art (which opened its doors originally on July 4, 2002), Florida Atlantic University, John D. MacArthur Campus, Jupiter, Florida

2001   Leonardo da Vinci World Award of Arts, the World Cultural Council, presented at Utrecht University, The Netherlands

2001   Women in the Visual Arts Lifetime Achievement Award, Delray Beach, Florida

2001   (Feb 26) EDNA HIBEL WAY Street-Naming Dedication, Jupiter, Florida

2000   Unveiling of "The Heart and Conscience of America," commemorating the 200th Anniversary of the White House and the founding of Wshington, District of Columbia, a massive 48'x60' oil on canvas commissioned by the White House Historical Association

Humanitarian and Civic Awards, Honors and Tributes Continued

1999   Doctorate of Humanities, Northwood University, West Palm Beach, Florida

1998   International Humanitarian for Health Award, Project HOPE, unveiling of commissioned painting, "In Priase of Humanity," marking the 40th Anniversary of Project Hope

1998   International Artist Award, B'nai B'rith, Washington DC

1998   Honorary International Chairperson, Guild for International Invitational Piano Competitions, Palm Beach, Florida

1998   Doctorate of Fine Arts, Honoris Causa, Providence College, Providence, Rhode Island

1997   Edna Hibel Dining Hall Dedication, Cafe Joshua, West Palm Beach, Florida

1997   Edna Hibel Day, Newton, Massachusetts

1995   Doctorate of Humanities, Honoris Causa, Eureka College, Eureka, Illinois

Humanitarian and Civic Awards, Honors and Tributes Continued

1995   Edna Hibel Birthing Room Dedication, Women's Hospital, Baton Rouge, Louisiana

1990   Humanitarian Award, Very Special Arts of Palm Beach, Florida

1988   Doctorate of Humane Leters, Honoris Causa, Mount Saint Mary's College, Emmitsburg, Maryland; Doctorate of Humane Arts, Honoris Causa, Univesity for Peace, Escazu, Costa Rica

1987   Business Excellence Award, Palm Beach Chapter, National Association of Women Business Owners

1987   Myrtle Wreath Achievement Award, Florida Atlantic Region, Hadassah

1987   Humanitarian Award, Palm Beach Council, B'nai B'rith

1986   General William Booth Humanitarian Award, Salvation Army Association, Palm Beach, Florida

1986   Humanitarian Award, Florida State Association of B'nai B'rith, Miami

1985   Presidential Award, Very Special Arts, Columbia
        University, New York City, New York, the first for
        someone other than a U.S. President

1984   Distinguished Humanitarian Award, Academy of
        Collectible Art, Los Angeles, California

1984   Included in *Who's Who and Why of Successful
        Florida Women*

1983   Diploma, Flanders Academy of Art, Science, and
        Letters, Belgium

1983   Honorary Citizenship, State of Alabama

1983   Honorary Citizenship, State of Tennessee

1983   Key to the City of New Orleans as Honorary
        Member, A Child's Wish of Greater New Orleans

1982   Commissioned a Kentucky Colonel as Honorary
        Citizen, Commonwealth of Kentucky

1982   Tribute, Northern New Jersey Hadassah, with
        Special Gratitude for Creativity and Dedication to
        Jewish Heritage through the Arts

1982   Blue Ribbon, Cordon Bleu de St. Esprit, Order of
        Frankreichs and the Maltese Cross, Cordon Bleu
        Society, France: Bestowed the rank of *Her
        Excellency, the Honorable Lady Edna,
        Commandeur*

1982	Humanitarian of the Year Spirit of Life Award, Palm Beach, Florida, Chapter, City of Hope
1982	Tribute, Florida Mid-Coast Region, Hadassah
1982	Award of Recognition, Chapter 188, Council for Exceptional Children, Orange County, California
1981	Honorary Citizenship, City of New Orleans, Louisiana
1981	Tribute, New Orleans Chapter, Hadassah, for Artistic Achievement and Humanitarian Concern
1980	Tribute, West Palm Beach, Florida, Chapter, Hadassah
1979	International Year of the Child Award, State of New Jersey
1979	Award of Appreciation, Israel Institute of Technology
1978	Torch of Learning Award, American Friends of the Hebrew University, New York City, New York
1976	Citizen Award, New England Region, Hadassah
1967	Included in *Who's Who of American Women*
1954	Included in *Who's Who in America*
1954	Founder, Boston Arts Festival, Massachusetts

1939   Ruth Sturtevant Traveling Fellowship, Boston
        Museum School of Fine Arts, to travel and paint in
        Mexico